Healthy Living

# Grains

by Vanessa Black

Bullfrog Books

# Ideas for Parents and Teachers

Bullfrog Books let children practice reading informational text at the earliest reading levels. Repetition, familiar words, and photo labels support early readers.

## Before Reading

- Discuss the cover photo. What does it tell them?
- Look at the picture glossary together. Read and discuss the words.

## Read the Book

- "Walk" through the book and look at the photos. Let the child ask questions. Point out the photo labels.
- Read the book to the child, or have him or her read independently.

## After Reading

- Prompt the child to think more. Ask: How many servings of grain do you eat a day? What is your favorite product made from grain?

Bullfrog Books are published by Jump!
5357 Penn Avenue South
Minneapolis, MN 55419
www.jumplibrary.com



Library of Congress Cataloging-in-Publication Data

Names: Black, Vanessa, author.
Title: Grains / by Vanessa Black.
Description: Minneapolis, MN: Jump!, Inc. [2016]
Series: Healthy living | "Bullfrog Books are published by Jump!" | Audience: Ages 5–8.
Audience: K to grade 3.
Includes bibliographical references and index.
Identifiers: LCCN 2016028287 (print)
LCCN 2016029217 (ebook)
ISBN 9781620315453 (hardcover: alk. paper)
ISBN 9781620315804 (pbk.)
ISBN 9781624964930 (ebook)
Subjects: LCSH: Grain in human nutrition
Juvenile literature. | Grain—Juvenile literature.
Nutrition—Juvenile literature.
Health—Juvenile literature.
Classification: LCC QP144.G73 B53 2016 (print)
LCC QP144.G73 (ebook) | DDC 641.3/31—dc23
LC record available at https://lccn.loc.gov/2016028287

Editor: Jenny Fretland VanVoorst
Book Designer: Molly Ballanger
Photo Researcher: Molly Ballanger

Photo Credits: All photos by Shutterstock except: Getty, 14–15, 16, 23tl, 23mr; iStock, 17.

Printed in the United States of America at Corporate Graphics in North Mankato, Minnesota.

## Table of Contents

# Good Food

Ed wants a snack.

Pop! Pop!
He makes popcorn.
Corn is a grain.

So is wheat.

So are oats and rice.

rice
oats
wheat

A grain is a seed.

It comes from a plant.

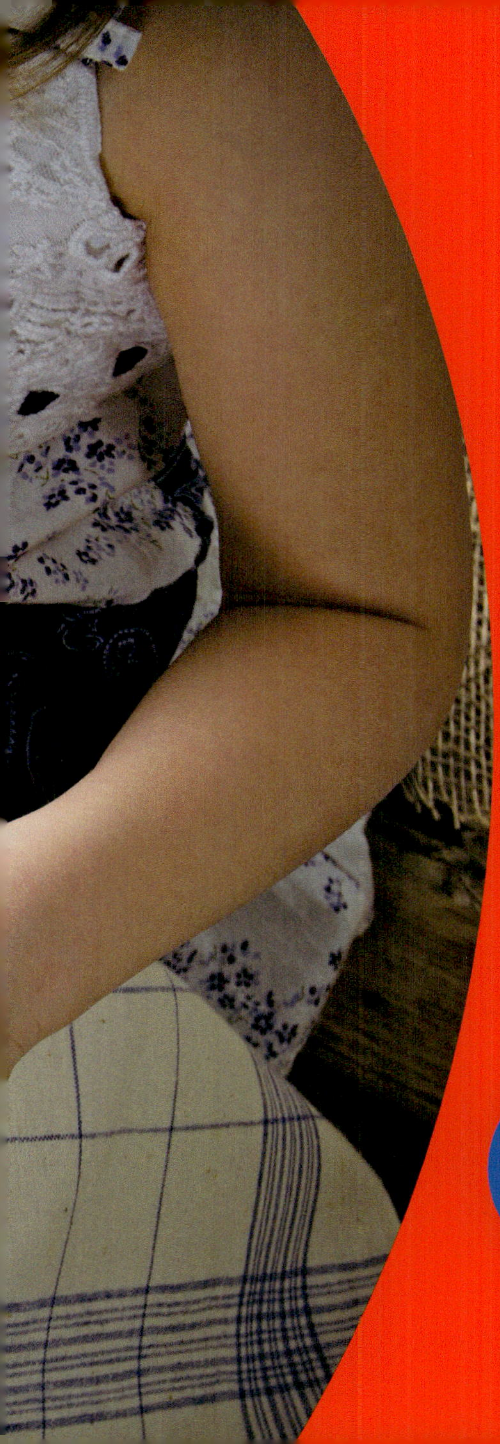

Grains have fiber.
It helps you digest.
They have iron.
It helps your heart.

Whole grains are best.
They taste good, too.

corn
tortilla

Ada has a tortilla.

It is made from corn.

Cal has a bagel.
It is made from wheat.

Tia has a cookie.
It is made with oats.

rice
noodles

Mo has noodles.

They are made from rice.

Grains are good food.

Yum!

# Your Daily Grains

**You need five servings of grains a day. Three servings should be whole grains.**

**whole grain bread**
Whole grain bread is most healthful because it contains nutrients from all parts of the grain.

**white rice**
White rice is less healthful than brown rice because nutrients from part of the kernel have been removed.

**pasta**
Pasta is made from flour, a powder made of ground-up wheat, rice, or other grain.

**buckwheat**
Buckwheat is a kind of wheat; it is an important ingredient in Eastern European cooking.

# Picture Glossary

**bagel**
A ring-shaped bread made from wheat flour.

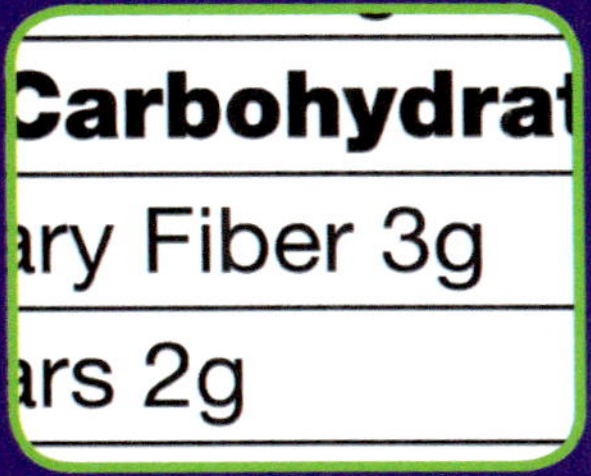


**fiber**
Part of a grain that helps you digest food.

**iron**
A mineral that your body needs to stay healthy.

**seed**
The part of a plant that is capable of producing a new plant.

**tortilla**
A soft, thin flatbread made from corn or wheat flour.

**whole grains**
Foods made using the whole kernel of a grain.

# Index

# To Learn More

Learning more is as easy as 1, 2, 3.

1) Go to www.factsurfer.com

2) Enter "grains" into the search box.

3) Click the "Surf" button to see a list of websites.

With factsurfer.com, finding more information is just a click away.